The Curious Little Kitten
Around the

By Linda Hayward
Illustrated by Maggie Swanson

A Golden Book · New York
Western Publishing Company, Inc.
Racine, Wisconsin 53404

There was once a little kitten who was born in a dark, cozy closet. She knew everything in there.

She knew her mother's soft, warm fur. She knew her brothers' tiny, hungry meows. She knew how the light looked when it came through the open door.

But one day she became curious about the light that came through the open door. She wondered, Where is that light coming from? And what *else* is on the other side of that door?

Her mother was taking a nap. *Pit pat, pit pat*, out the closet door went the curious little kitten.

On the other side of the closet door, it was dark. The
light was gone.

The curious little kitten was standing in a little girl's
bedroom. The bedroom was full of things she had never
seen before—a bed, a lamp, a fuzzy slipper.

The kitten wondered, What was shining so brightly
before?

She looked at the bed, at the lamp, at the fuzzy slipper.

Then the curious little kitten heard a loud ringing sound. RINGGG-RINGGG-RINGGG! She saw another door. The sound was coming through the door.

She was curious about that sound. She wondered, What is making the ringing sound? And what *else* is on the other side of that door?

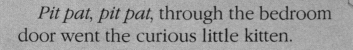
Pit pat, *pit pat*, through the bedroom door went the curious little kitten.

On the other side of the door, it was quiet. The ringing had stopped.

The curious little kitten was standing in a hallway. The hallway was full of things she had never seen before—a table, a telephone, a red rubber ball.

The kitten wondered, What was ringing so loudly just now?

She looked at the table, at the telephone, at the red rubber ball.

The curious little kitten pushed the red rubber ball with her paw. SWISH! The red rubber ball rolled down the hallway and right off the end of the floor!

The little kitten was *very* curious.

At the end of the floor were some steps.

PLOP, PLOP, PLOP, down the steps bounced the red rubber ball.

Plip, plip, plip, down the steps went the curious little kitten.

From the bottom, the steps looked different. They went up.

Now the curious little kitten was standing in a nice comfortable living room. The living room was full of things she had never seen before—a couch, a fireplace, a tall ticking clock.

The kitten wondered, Where is the red rubber ball?

She looked under the couch, in the fireplace, behind the tall ticking clock.

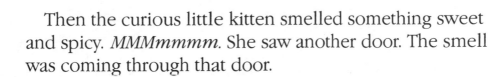

Then the curious little kitten smelled something sweet
and spicy. *MMMmmmm.* She saw another door. The smell
was coming through that door.

She was curious about the smell. She wondered, What
smells so good? And what *else* is on the other side of that
door?

Pit pat, pit pat, through the door went the curious little
kitten.

On the other side of the door, the sweet and spicy smell seemed even sweeter and spicier.

The curious little kitten was standing in a small cheerful kitchen. The kitchen was full of things she had never seen before—a chair, a pie, a blue-and-white-checked tablecloth.

The kitten wondered, Now *what* could smell so delicious?

She patted the blue-and-white-checked tablecloth with her paw. Here was something soft!

She pounced around the edge of it. Here was something that didn't roll away!

FLOOP! The blue-and-white-checked tablecloth slid right off the table and landed on the curious little kitten.

She was trapped. She was scared. She wanted to be back in her own dark, cozy, safe closet.

"Mew, mew, mew," went the curious little kitten.

Then she heard her mother's friendly meow. She felt her mother's soft, warm fur.

Through the kitchen, through the living room, and up the stairs went the curious little kitten.

Through the hallway and into the bedroom went the curious little kitten.

Her mother carried her all the way back to the dark, cozy closet where she knew everything.

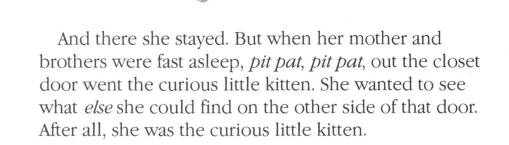

And there she stayed. But when her mother and brothers were fast asleep, *pit pat, pit pat*, out the closet door went the curious little kitten. She wanted to see what *else* she could find on the other side of that door. After all, she was the curious little kitten.